MONEY DOESN'T GROW ON MARS

For Mom, with love—L.H.H.

**For John, an amazing being who teaches
me about Earth money—J.W.**

Text copyright © 2017 by Lori Haskins Houran
Illustrations copyright © 2017 by Jessica Warrick
Galaxy Scout Activities illustrations copyright © 2017 by Kane Press, Inc.
Galaxy Scout Activities illustrations by Nadia DiMattia

Library of Congress Cataloging-in-Publication Data

Names: Houran, Lori Haskins, author. | Warrick, Jessica, illustrator.
Title: Money doesn't grow on Mars / by Lori Haskins Houran ;
illustrated by Jessica Warrick.
Description: New York : The Kane Press, 2017. | Series: How to be an
earthling ; 8 | Summary: "Jack takes various jobs to earn money for a
special comic, but finds out spending money is easier than saving it"—
Provided by publisher.
Identifiers: LCCN 2016029835| ISBN 9781575658506 (pbk) |
ISBN 9781575658469 (reinforced library binding) | ISBN 9781575658544 (ebook)
Subjects: | CYAC: Extraterrestrial beings—Fiction. | Money—Fiction. |
Humorous stories.
Classification: LCC PZ7.H27645 Mo 2017 | DDC [Fic]—dc23
LC record available at https://lccn.loc.gov/2016029835

1 3 5 7 9 10 8 6 4 2

First published in the United States of America in 2017 by Kane Press, Inc.
Printed in China

Book Design: Edward Miller

How to Be an Earthling is a registered trademark of Kane Press, Inc.

Visit us online at **www.kanepress.com**

Like us on Facebook
facebook.com/kanepress

Follow us on Twitter
@KanePress

CONTENTS

Don't miss a single one
of Spork's adventures!

MONEY DOESN'T GROW ON MARS

by Lori Haskins Houran
illustrated by Jessica Warrick

KANE PRESS
New York

Grace Hanford

Piper Cho

Adam Novak

Newton Miller

Jo Jo

GALAXY SCOUTS

BEEP. BEEP. BEEP.

Guys! Are you there? Sorry I'm late! I just found the most awesome thing on Earth. Video games! Newton let me borrow one, and I've been playing it for two Earth hours. Oops, make that four Earth hours! That's why this report is a teensy bit late.

Anyway, I think we should make video games on OUR planet! So I'll keep playing this one—you know, for research. In fact, I'll get back to it right now.

BYE!

1

TALONS AND FIRE

Jack's eyes were wide. His mouth hung open.

"No drooling on the comics," teased Nina. "Especially that one."

Jack held a comic book in his hands. Not just any comic book. A rare Talons and Fire—from the very first year they were made. He'd never seen one in person before!

"Wh-when did you get this?" asked Jack.

"Just this morning." Nina finished dusting a shelf. "Isn't it great?"

"Amazing," whispered Jack.

Jack could just picture it in his collection. He'd build a special display case for it, with a spotlight shining on the cover. . . .

Jack had been collecting Talons and Fire comics forever. He always bought them at Nina's shop, Colossal Comics. Nina was the only one he could talk to about T and F. Everyone else's eyes glazed over whenever he brought it up—which he just didn't get. How could people not be into a world ruled by dragons and danger and destiny?

Jack turned over the comic and looked at the price tag. Twenty dollars? Oof!

A regular T and F cost two dollars, and he had a hard time coming up with that. Usually he dug under the cushions in the living room couch. But twenty bucks? He'd never find that much.

He put the comic back on the shelf. But he couldn't stop staring at it.

"So, Jack," said Nina, "I was just thinking. I'm getting tired of dusting shelves. How'd you like to help me out on Saturday mornings? I could pay you five dollars a week."

Jack gasped. "Really? Then I could save up for the Talons and Fire!"

"Sure," Nina said. "And if you like, I could hang onto it for you while you earn the money."

"Awesome!" shouted Jack.

"I can only hold it for a month, though," Nina added. "Then I'll have to put it up for sale again. Deal?"

"Deal!" Jack said. He shook Nina's hand.

"See you next week!" she said.

Jack practically bounced along the sidewalk. As he passed Betsy's Diner, he saw Betsy out front with a broom.

"Good morning!" said Jack.

"Morning, Jack! Just finished my Saturday sweeping," Betsy explained. "I always have to do it fast so I don't burn my muffins!"

BING! An idea popped into Jack's brain.

"Hey, would you like some help?" he asked. "I'm going to be working at Colossal on Saturdays, and I have plenty of time for another job. I could sweep your sidewalk for you."

"Jack, that would be lovely! I'll give you two dollars a week. And how about a bonus blueberry muffin right now?"

Jack polished off the muffin as he continued down the street. He stopped at the market on the corner.

"Can I help you?" the manager asked. The nametag on his shirt said "Hector."

"I was hoping I could help you, sir,"
said Jack. He told Hector about his jobs
at the diner and the comic shop.

"Tell you what," said Hector. "I always
have a stack of boxes to recycle on
Saturday mornings. If you carry them to
the curb for me, I'll pay you a dollar."

Jack couldn't believe it. Five dollars at Colossal, two dollars at Betsy's, and now a dollar at the market. Eight dollars a week! At that rate, he could buy the Talons and Fire in three weeks, not four—with money to spare!

Jack grinned. Soon he'd own the coolest comic in the world.

2

SPACE RACER

"I got three jobs this weekend!" Jack announced at school first thing Monday morning. "I'm going to use the money to buy a rare Talons and Fire!"

"Oh, Talons and Fire. That's nice, Jack," said Piper.

Jack saw her eyes glaze over . . . as always.

So did Newton's and Trixie's.

Only Spork's didn't. But that was just because something else was going on with the little alien's eyes. They looked weird. Sort of twirly.

"What did you do this weekend, Spork?" asked Trixie.

"I played Space Racer," said Spork. "It was cosmic! My ship kept winning!"

"How can you get excited about that

video game?" Trixie asked. "Don't you fly real spaceships? In actual outer space?"

"Yes," said Spork. "But this is different. There are levels, and points, and secret tricks to earn more points. It's so much fun that . . . it's hard to stop playing."

Spork's hands were twitching a bit, as if he were still pressing the buttons on the video game controller. His eyes were still twirling, too.

"Are you okay?" Newton asked him.

"Sure," said Spork. "I'm flying. I mean, I'm fine."

Jack saw Newton give Trixie a worried look. He sighed. Why was everyone always fussing over Spork?

Ever since the alien landed on the playground a few months ago, it seemed as if he got all the attention. First Mrs. Buckle invited him to join the class. Then kids kept going out of their way to help him.

When is Spork going to stop needing help, anyway? thought Jack. Then he noticed something. Spork's eyes weren't the only things twirling. His head started making slow circles, too.

Suddenly the alien's feet lifted off the ground. His whole body began turning cartwheels in the air. He looked like a Spork-sized pinwheel!

"Spork! Are you okay?" yelled Piper.

"Space Racer," Spork said in a flat voice. "SPACE. RACER!"

"My goodness!" cried Mrs. Buckle, running over. "Jack, please take Spork straight to the nurse's office!"

"Come on, Spork," Jack grumbled. He nudged the orange alien down the hall, tapping his ankle now and then to keep him spinning in the right direction.

Jack knocked on the nurse's door. "Mr. Greg?"

"Yikes!" said Mr. Greg, moving a lamp out of Spork's way. "What's going on?"

Jack explained that Spork started acting funny after he told the class about playing Space Racer all weekend.

"I'll bet that's the problem," said Mr. Greg. "When we humans eat too much junk food, we get a stomachache. When Spork plays too many video games, his body reacts, too. He just needs time to recover. I'll keep him here for a while. Thanks, Jack."

Shaking his head, Jack headed to Mrs. Buckle's room. Who would play a game so much they wound up in the nurse's office? Spork was out of control!

After lunch, Spork came back to class. He was walking, not spinning.

"Spork! It's good to see you back to normal!" said Mrs. Buckle. "Are you okay?"

"Yes. But I can't play Space Racer so much anymore," Spork said sadly. "Mr. Greg says I should only play it thirty minutes a day."

Jack rolled his eyes. "Big deal," he muttered. "Get a grip."

Mrs. Buckle raised an eyebrow at Jack. Then she looked back at Spork.

"Sometimes it can be hard to 'get a grip,'" she said. "Especially when we really like something. Have I told you all how much I love old movies?"

"James Bond movies, right?" said Newton.

Mrs. Buckle nodded. "When I first

became a teacher, I used to stay up late watching them. One morning, after a very late night, I fell asleep in the middle of teaching math."

"No!" gasped Grace.

"After that, I realized I needed self-control. I had to make myself go to bed at a reasonable hour," Mrs. Buckle said. "Everybody needs self-control sometimes, but for different reasons. For you it might be about playing video games, or drinking soda, or texting your friends. There isn't always someone to tell you when to stop, so you have to learn to set limits for yourself."

"That doesn't sound like much fun," said Trixie.

"I know," Mrs. Buckle said. "But it's a good thing. After all, who wants to drool in front of an entire class?"

"Ew!" Jack said. "Did you really drool?"

"Right on my desk," said Mrs. Buckle.

Gross! thought Jack.

Jack got what Mrs. Buckle was saying. But it didn't mean much to him. He didn't stay up too late, or play too many video games, or do too much of anything. He didn't need to get a grip.

He was in complete control.

3

EVEN SWEETER

I don't know why grown-ups complain about work, thought Jack the next Saturday. *It's so much better than school!*

He whistled while he swept Betsy's sidewalk. He hummed while he stacked boxes at the market. And he smiled as he pushed open the door to Colossal. This was the job he'd looked forward to the most!

"Hey, Jack! Now, where did I put the stuff for you?"

Nina found a spray bottle and a cloth. "Will you start with the shelves in the back? I haven't gotten to those in a while."

Nina wasn't kidding. The back shelves were coated with gray fuzz. Jack took the comics off the lowest shelf and started cleaning.

"Ah-choo!"

A few squirts, a few wipes, and a few sneezes later, the shelf was shiny. Jack started putting back the comics.

Hmm—he'd never seen some of them before. Sarton's Scales? Wings of Winter? The dragons on the covers looked pretty cool. Not quite as cool as Talons and Fire, of course!

Jack moved on to the next shelf, and the next, and the next.

After an hour, Nina came walking back.

"Super job!" she said. "You can tackle more shelves next week. Come up front and I'll pay you."

"Okay."

At the cash register, Jack handed Nina the cleaning supplies, and she passed him five crisp dollar bills.

Jack stepped out into the sunshine, feeling great. He patted his pocket. There was a fat lump of bills there!

Jack glanced across the street. He saw an "Open" sign on The Sweet Spot candy store.

Oooh. A Gooey Chewy would taste so good right now.

Jack patted his full pocket again. Why not get himself a little treat?

Inside the store, Jack slid a candy bar across the counter. He grabbed a can of soda, too. He handed the clerk two dollars and headed home, ripping open the Gooey Chewy along the way.

YUM! Was it his imagination . . . or did candy bought with his own money taste even sweeter than usual?

The next Saturday was just as much fun as the first—even if Jack didn't discover any unusual comics this time, just a bunch of regular old Batmans and Supermans.

After work, Jack stopped by The Sweet Spot for another Gooey Chewy and a soda. Next to the checkout counter he spied a jar marked PRANK YOUR PALS! Instead of candy, it was filled with trick toys.

Jack fished a joy buzzer out of the jar. "Give your friends a handshake that's truly shocking!" read the tag.

Jack smiled. He could just imagine zapping Newton!

He looked at the tag again. The buzzer was three dollars. Should he get it?

If he did, he wasn't sure he'd have enough money left to buy the Talons and Fire next week. He really liked the idea of buying it a week early.

Then again, Nina had agreed to hold the comic for four weeks. He could still buy it on time . . . and have the joy buzzer, too. That made sense, right? Besides, the look on Newton's face would be so funny!

Chuckling to himself, Jack put the extra three dollars on the counter.

Back home, he stuffed the rest of the bills in his piggy bank. Then he lay back on his pillow, daydreaming about Talons and Fire.

4

SMASH!

"Greetings, Jack!" said Spork.

"What are you doing here?" Jack asked.

It was two Saturdays later. Jack was on his way to Betsy's Diner for his first job of the day. He carried his piggy bank carefully in both hands.

"Newton took his Space Racer game back," Spork said, "but I heard they have it at an arcade on Main Street.

Don't worry—I've only been playing thirty minutes a day, like Mr. Greg said."

"Oh. Hey, guess what?" said Jack, holding up the piggy bank. "Today's the day I buy the rare Talons and Fire!"

"Cosmic!" said Spork. Something across the street caught his eye. "THE ARCADE!" he squeaked. He sped off.

"Jeez," muttered Jack. "He was in a rush."

Jack wanted to rush, too. He couldn't wait to buy the comic! But he made himself slow down and do a good job at Betsy's.

"That sidewalk is so clean you could eat off it!" she declared, handing him two dollars. He stuffed them into the piggy bank.

Jack stacked ten boxes in front of the market and lined up the corners neatly. "Here you go," said Hector, and Jack stuck another bill into the bank.

Finally he got to Colossal. He dusted a dozen shelves before Nina called him up front.

"Ready?" she asked, handing him five dollars.

Jack stuffed the bills into his piggy bank. They barely fit!

"Ready!" he said. His voice was shaking.

"Good," said Nina. "I had a collector in here who really wanted that comic. But I told him I was saving it for someone until today."

Jack lifted his piggy bank. "May I?"

"Go for it!" Nina said.

SMASH! Jack broke open the piggy bank, and dollar bills fluttered onto the counter. He gathered them up and started counting out loud.

"One. Two. Three . . ."

He kept going until there were only three bills left.

"Fifteen. Sixteen. Seventeen."

Wait, WHAT? Seventeen?

He'd been working for four weeks. He'd made thirty-two dollars. How could he only have seventeen? That mean he'd spent . . . he subtracted in his head . . . fifteen dollars. How was that possible?

Jack's mind flashed back over the last four weeks. He remembered buying a few sodas. Some Gooey Chewy candy bars. The joy buzzer. Last week he'd picked up a pair of X-ray glasses and a can of silly string, too.

How could he have spent so much money on junk? He didn't even care about the dumb pranks. All he cared about was the comic book!

"I—I don't have enough," Jack said.

"Jack, I'm so sorry," Nina said gently. "I can't keep holding it."

"I understand," mumbled Jack. He jammed the seventeen dollars into his pocket and rushed outside, trying not to cry.

He started home. Then he swerved and shoved open the door of The Sweet Spot.

I already blew my chance at the Talons and Fire. Why not just blow the rest of my money?

Jack started piling stuff on the counter. A Gooey Chewy. A pack of trick gum. Fake doggy doo. He didn't even care what he was buying.

He kept piling until the cashier said, "That will be seventeen dollars."

Jack handed over all his bills, grabbed the shopping bag, and left.

Across the street, in the window of the arcade, something caught his eye. A small, orange something, hunched over a game. Spork!

So much for thirty minutes, Jack thought. *It's been way longer than that. Spork needs to get a gr—*

"Oh!" Suddenly it hit Jack. The way Spork played Space Racer wasn't so different from the way he spent money. They were both out of control. And they both needed to get a grip—right now!

Jack marched into the arcade. Spork's twirly eyes were glued to the video screen.

"Time to go, Spork," said Jack firmly.

"Can't. Go," said Spork. "More. Points."

Argh! *Now what?* thought Jack.

Jack reached into his bag. "Spork, have you ever had a Gooey Chewy?"

"Gooey. Chewy?" Spork's eyes flickered off the screen for just a second.

"It's the best candy bar in the galaxy," said Jack. "I'll let you have it if you come with me."

He ripped open the candy bar and waved it under Spork's nose.

"Keep. Playing," said Spork.

But he loosened his grip on the game controller.

Jack waved the candy bar again.

Spork stood up!

Wave by wave, Jack lured Spork outside. As soon as the fresh air hit Spork's face, he shook his head. He blinked a few times, and his eyes stopped twirling.

"Uh-oh. I did it again, didn't I? I played too long. Thank you for getting me out of there, Jack."

"Er, sure," said Jack. He wasn't used to helping Spork. It felt a little strange!

He thrust the candy bar at the alien. "Here."

"Thanks." Spork took a bite. "Cosmic! This IS the best candy bar in the galaxy. You really know what you're talking about!"

"Oh, yeah?" said Jack. He couldn't help smiling. "So, um, you know what else is awesome? Have you ever read Talons and Fire? There are these dragons. . . ."

5

COSMIC COMICS

Jack told Spork all about T and F while the alien ate the candy bar. To Jack's surprise, Spork's eyes didn't glaze over. He actually seemed interested!

"Aren't you buying one of those comics today?" Spork asked. "A special one?"

Jack's face fell. "Well—"

"Jack? Spork? Is that you?"

Jack looked up and saw Mr. Greg, the school nurse.

"I'm on my way to Colossal Comics," Mr. Greg explained. "They have a rare T and F—sorry, that stands for Talons and Fire. Anyway, it just became available, and I'm buying it for my collection!"

"Isn't that the one you're getting, Jack?" asked Spork.

Jack looked at the ground. He scuffed his feet.

"Wait," Mr. Greg said. "Jack, are you the person Nina was saving it for?"

"Yeah," muttered Jack, "but I messed up."

He told Mr. Greg the whole story. How he got three jobs to earn the money for the comic. How he spent too much instead of saving. How he got so upset, he blew the rest of the money. Every dollar!

"Oh, Jack," said Mr. Greg. "I know what it's like to miss out on your favorite comic. When I was a kid, all I wanted was a Wings of Winter, but I could never find one. Not one! I only started collecting Talons and Fire because I couldn't get Wings of Winter."

"Wings of Winter?" said Jack. "But there's one in Nina's shop."

"SERIOUSLY?" shouted Mr. Greg. He took off in a sprint toward Colossal!

Jack and Spork hurried to catch up.

Inside, Nina followed them to the back of the shop.

"Here it is," Jack said.

"Amazing," whispered Mr. Greg.

"I had no idea that was back here," said Nina. "Jack, you're obviously a better duster than I am!"

"Now what, Mr. Greg?" asked Spork. "Are you still going to buy the Talons and Fire?"

Mr. Greg thought for a minute. "Yes," he said. "I'm buying both comics."

Jack's heart sank.

"BUT," Mr. Greg continued, "if Jack saves twenty dollars in the next three weeks, I'll sell him the T and F. Otherwise, it stays in my collection for good."

"Thank you, Mr. Greg!" said Jack. "I can do it. I know I can!"

Jack worked even harder than usual the next three Saturdays. Every time he passed The Sweet Spot, he told himself, "Get a grip. Get a grip!"

He didn't buy any soda. Or popcorn. Or trick toys. (Not even a squirting flower that Trixie would totally fall for.)

He did buy a Gooey Chewy, but that was okay. He was keeping track of his money this time. He knew he could afford it.

On the last Saturday, Jack knocked on Spork's spaceship.

"Look!" he said proudly. "The rare Talons and Fire. I got it!"

"COSMIC!" Spork squeaked, jumping up and down.

"Hang on," Jack said. "Spork, why do your eyes look twirly? Have you been playing too much Space Racer again?"

"Nope! Not since you let me borrow your collection of T and F comics. They're so good, I've been staying up all night reading them!"

"All night?" said Jack. "Oh, boy . . ."

REPORT TO TROOP

BEEP. BEEP. BEEP.
Guys, I found something
even BETTER than video games
for our planet. Comic books! There's
this series, Talons and Fire, about a
bunch of dragons—
ZZZT.
Hey, where'd you go? Did someone hit
"End Transmission" by mistake? So anyway,
it's a world ruled by dragons and danger
and—
ZZZT.
Guys? Hello? HELLO?

Greetings!
Talons and Fire is a cosmic comic book series. I have to save my money for the next issue. But glarps!—that means no Space Racer at the arcade. That's going to be tough. Can you help me? Do you have self-control? Take this Galactic Self-Control Survey to find out.
—Spork

(There can be more than one right answer.)

1. There's a lot of moondust cake left over after your Galaxy Scout meeting. How can you show self-control?
   a. Ask for a piece to take back to your spaceship.
   b. Eat just the icing. Take that, self-control!
   c. Tell all your friends to try it. If there's any left over, maybe you'll have a second piece.
   d. Grab another Jupiter-sized slice and dig in—YUM!

2. Your mom gave you money for a week of lunches at Scout Camp. On your way to camp you pass the arcade. What do you do?
   a. Stop in and play just one game.
   b. Spend all of your money at the arcade. You'll skip lunch this week.
   c. Buy snacks instead of lunch and save the extra money for the arcade.
   d. Ask your mom if you can use any leftover money at the end of the week to play Space Racer.

3. You're having fun building your own galaxy in the new AstroCraft game, but it's almost bedtime. You:

   a. Turn the clocks back an hour so your parents don't know it's bedtime.

   b. Ask your parents for a later bedtime.

   c. Turn off the game, set an early alarm, and play before school.

   d. Set a timer for ten more minutes and stop playing when the timer goes off.

4. Zorp isn't allowed to ride his kickleride past the end of his street. But he sees some of his Scout friends a block away. What should he do?

   a. Yell and ask his friends to zoom closer.

   b. See if a neighbor on his street can play.

   c. Cross the street—it's only a little farther.

   d. Pretend he forgot the rule and take a long ride with his friends.

Answers:

1. Resisting the temptation to immediately stuff yourself with cake is a good way of showing self-control, so *a* and *c* are good choices. *B* is a step in the right direction, but don't leave any icing-less cake for others—that's just mean! Choose *d* and you could get a Jupiter-sized tummy ache.

2. Playing just one game does show some self-control, so *a* is a fine answer—but the money was for lunch, so you should check with your mom first. That makes *d* a better answer. And don't choose *b* or *c*. Growing bodies need healthy meals, so skipping lunch or just eating snacks isn't healthy.

3. Your brain and body need a good night's sleep, so choose *d* or you'll be flarg-tired in the morning! C is okay only if you're sure to get enough sleep. It's always good to check with your parents, but *a* and *b* aren't the best choices for sleepy young aliens.

4. Adults make rules to keep Earth kids and alien kids safe, so not crossing the street is very important. A and *b* are good choices. C and *d* are not.

Space Facts: True or False

My Galaxy Scout leaders haven't stopped sending me pop quizzes just because I've been living on Earth! They say I have to keep my Scouting skills sharp. Try the latest quiz and see how you do.

1. Astronauts' footprints will stay on the moon for about 100 years before blowing away.
2. A sunset on Mars is blue.
3. Pluto is no longer a planet because a black hole sucked it up.
4. The moon is slowly drifting away from Earth.
5. If you put Saturn in water it would float.
6. The Milky Way is home to a cow-shaped nebula that's a million light years wide.

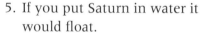

Answers:

1. False. The footprints could actually stay there for 100 *million* years! There's no wind on the moon to wipe them out.
2. True. Dust in the air on Mars scatters red light, so there's a bluish glow around the sun when it sets.
3. False. There are no black holes near our solar system. And Pluto is doing just fine—even if it's not a planet anymore.
4. True, but don't worry—it only drifts about 1.5 inches a year!
5. True. Saturn is huge, but it isn't very dense. That means it would float in a *ginormous* pool of water.
6. False. Scientists have not discovered a giant cow-shaped nebula. Yet. (The Horsehead Nebula, however, is quite a sight!)

Spork's Space Jokes

Q: What do planets like to read?
A: Comet books!

MEET THE AUTHOR AND ILLUSTRATOR

LORI HASKINS HOURAN
has written more than twenty books for kids (not counting the ones her flarg ate). She lives in Florida with two silly aliens who claim to be her sons.

JESSICA WARRICK has illustrated lots of picture books about dogs, cats, and kids, but she is mostly interested in drawing aliens, for some strange reason. She does a pretty good job acting like an Earthling . . . most of the time.

Spork just landed on Earth, and look, he already has lots of fans!

★ **Moonbeam Children's Book Awards Gold Medal**
Best Book Series—Chapter Books

★ **Moonbeam Children's Book Awards Silver Medal**
Juvenile Fiction—Early Reader/Chapter Books
for book #1 *Spork Out of Orbit*

"Young readers are going to love this series! Spork is a funny and unexpected main character. Kids will love his antics and sweet disposition. Teachers and parents will appreciate the subtle messages embedded in the stories. The kids in the stories genuinely like each other, which I found refreshing. I will be giving these books to my young friends."—**Ron Roy**, author of A to Z Mysteries, Calendar Mysteries, and Capital Mysteries

"A breezy, humorous lesson in honesty that never stoops to didacticism. The other three volumes publishing simultaneously address similarly weighty lessons—lying, shyness, bullying, and responsibility—all with a multicultural cast of Everykids. . . . A good choice for those new to chapters."
—**Kirkus** for book #1 *Spork Out of Orbit*

"This is a book where readers, kids, and aliens learn together, experiencing how words and choices affect all of us. It's simple, elegant, and very insightful storytelling. *Greetings, Sharkling!* doesn't waste a single page of opportunity."
—**The San Francisco Book Review**

"I'm so glad Spork landed on Earth! His misadventures are playful and sweet, and I love the clever wordplay!"
—**Becca Zerkin**, former children's book reviewer for the *New York Times Book Review* and *School Library Journal*

"Kids will love reading about Spork. Parents, teachers, and librarians will love reading aloud this series to those same kids."—**Rob Reid**, author of *Silly Books to Read Aloud*

How to Be an Earthling
Winner of the Moonbeam Gold Medal
for Best Chapter Book Series!

Respect

Honesty

Responsibility

Courage

Kindness

Perseverance

Citizenship

Self-Control

To learn more about Spork, go to kanepress.com

Check out these other series from Kane Press

Animal Antics A to Z®
(Grades PreK–2 • Ages 3–8)
Winner of two *Learning* Magazine Teachers' Choice Awards
"A great product for any class learning about letters!"
—*Teachers' Choice Award reviewer comment*

Let's Read Together®
(Grades PreK–3 • Ages 4–8)
"Storylines are silly and inventive, and recall Dr. Seuss's *Cat in the Hat*
for the building of rhythm and rhyming words."—*School Library Journal*

Holidays & Heroes
(Grades 1–4 • Ages 6–10)
"Commemorates the influential figures behind important American
celebrations. This volume emphasizes the importance of lofty ambitions
and fortitude in the face of adversity…"—*Booklist* (for *Let's Celebrate Martin
Luther King Jr. Day*)

Math Matters®
(Grades K–3 • Ages 5–8)
Winner of a *Learning* Magazine Teachers' Choice Award
"These cheerfully illustrated titles offer primary-grade
children practice in math as well as reading."—*Booklist*

The Milo & Jazz Mysteries®
(Grades 2–5 • Ages 7–11)
"Gets it just right."—*Booklist*, starred review (for *The Case
of the Stinky Socks*); *Book Links'* Best New Books for the Classroom

Mouse Math®
(Grades PreK & up • Ages 4 & up)
"The Mouse Math series is a great way to integrate math and literacy into
your early childhood curriculum. My students thoroughly enjoyed these
books."—*Teaching Children Mathematics*

Science Solves It!®
(Grades K–3 • Ages 5–8)
"The Science Solves It! series is a wonderful tool for
the elementary teacher who wants to integrate reading
and science."—*National Science Teachers Association*

Social Studies Connects®
(Grades K–3 • Ages 5–8)
"This series is very strongly recommended…."—*Children's Bookwatch*
"Well done!"—*School Library Journal*

KANEPRESS.com